My Secret Unicorn

Snowy Dreams

Twilight's magic was fading! Lauren
couldn't believe it. No more magic. No
more flying. And maybe soon, no more
talking to her best friend.
But the worst thing of all was how
unhappy this was making Twilight. Did he
really think she wouldn't love him
anymore, just because he wasn't a
unicorn?

My Secret Unicorn

Snowy Dreams

Linda Chapman

Illustrated by Ann Kronheimer

PUFFIN BOOKS

PUFFIN BOOKS

Published by the Penguin Group
Penguin Books Ltd, 80 Strand, London WC2R 0RL, England
Penguin Group (USA) Inc., 375 Hudson Street, New York, New York 10014, USA
Penguin Group (Canada), 90 Eglinton Avenue East, Suite 700, Toronto, Ontario, Canada M4P 2Y3
(a division of Pearson Penguin Canada Inc.)
Penguin Ireland, 25 St Stephen's Green, Dublin 2, Ireland (a division of Penguin Books Ltd)
Penguin Group (Australia), 250 Camberwell Road, Camberwell, Victoria 3124, Australia
(a division of Pearson Australia Group Pty Ltd)
Penguin Books India Pvt Ltd, 11 Community Centre, Panchsheel Park,
New Delhi – 110 017, India
Penguin Group (NZ), cnr Airborne and Rosedale Roads, Albany, Auckland 1310, New Zealand
(a division of Pearson New Zealand Ltd)
Penguin Books (South Africa) (Pty) Ltd, 24 Sturdee Avenue, Rosebank,
Johannesburg 2196, South Africa

Penguin Books Ltd, Registered Offices: 80 Strand, London WC2R 0RL, England

www.penguin.com

First published 2005
1

Text copyright © Working Partners Ltd, 2005
Illustrations copyright © Ann Kronheimer, 2005
All rights reserved

The moral right of the author and illustrator has been asserted

Set in 14.25/21.5pt Bembo
Made and printed in England by Clays Ltd, St Ives plc

British Library Cataloguing in Publication Data
A CIP catalogue record for this book is available from the British Library

ISBN-13: 978-0-141-32026-5
ISBN-10: 0-141-32026-5

To Jessica Duxbury, a very special friend

Prologue

In a distant land, three Unicorn Elders
stood beside a stone table. Their silvery
manes swept to the floor and their snow-
white coats gleamed in the moonlight.
One had a golden horn, one had a silver
and the third had a bronze.

'It is time for us to find out,' the silver-
horned unicorn said softly.

The other two unicorns nodded their

noble heads.

The first unicorn touched the table top with her silver horn. Purple smoke began to drift across the surface and the stone shone like a mirror. An image appeared. It showed a small grey pony grazing in a field near a farmhouse at night-time. Behind the farm, almost hidden in shadow, rose the Blue Ridge Mountains of Virginia.

'It's Twilight,' the bronze-horned unicorn said slowly.

The three unicorns exchanged looks.

'I am surprised,' remarked the unicorn with the golden horn. 'Twilight is very young.' His voice sounded troubled.

The bronze-horned unicorn nodded.

'He is, and he has not been with his unicorn friend for long. But they have done many good things together – more than some unicorns and their friends do in many years.'

'That is true.' The unicorn with the golden horn looked at the others. 'I wonder how Twilight will take the news.'

'It is never easy,' the silver-horned unicorn said quietly. Her dark eyes, shimmering like deep pools, watched Twilight for a moment. 'I will go and tell him.'

'When will you go, Sidra?' the other unicorns asked.

Sidra lifted her head, her horn glittering in the starlight. 'Tonight.'

CHAPTER
One

Beep-beep-beep! Lauren Foster rubbed her eyes. Her alarm clock went off again. *Beep-beep-beep!* Fumbling at the side of her bed, she pressed the off-switch on the clock then sank back against her pillows. *What day is it?* she wondered sleepily.

Saturday! And not just any old Saturday but the first day of the Christmas holidays! Lauren suddenly felt wide awake. She didn't have to go to school for over two whole weeks and she could spend every day with Twilight!

Jumping out of bed, she padded over to the window. Pulling the curtains open, she saw Twilight standing by his paddock gate and she smiled. The day she had got Twilight had been the best day of her life. *Well*, *almost*, she thought, remembering the time a few weeks after that when she had found out that Twilight wasn't just an ordinary pony – he was a secret unicorn! Now, when Lauren's parents and little brother, Max, were sleeping, she turned Twilight into his magical unicorn shape so that they

could go flying and do good deeds using his magical powers. Lauren knew she was really lucky to have a pony, and she was even luckier to have a unicorn as well!

Twilight began to walk along by the fence. Reaching the end of the field, he turned and paced back again. Lauren frowned. It wasn't like Twilight to be so restless. He usually waited patiently by the gate. *He must be hungry*, she decided.

Turning from the window, she pulled on her jeans and warm sweatshirt. As she got dressed, she planned the morning in her head. She'd feed Twilight his breakfast and then groom him. At nine thirty, Mel and Jessica, her two best friends, were coming over on their ponies to go for a ride in the woods. The weekend before, the three of them had discovered a large clearing in the trees with banks and steep slopes. They'd had great fun riding there and had decided to go back again.

Today's going to be brilliant! Lauren thought. Tying her long fair hair back in a ponytail, she hurried downstairs.

The rest of the house was quiet. Her
dad's boots weren't on the porch so
Lauren guessed he was out working on
the family's farm. Buddy, Max's young
Bernese mountain dog, jumped up when
he saw her. She stopped to scratch his
ears. 'Max will be up soon,' she told him.

Buddy wagged his tail and licked her
hand. Grabbing an apple from the bowl,
Lauren ran out of the house and down
the frosty path to Twilight's field.

'Twilight!' she called.

Twilight stopped walking and looked
round.

'Hi, boy!'

Whinnying, Twilight trotted to the

gate. When he reached it, he pushed his head against her, almost knocking her over.

'Steady!' Lauren laughed. 'Yes, the apple's for you. Here you go.'

But to her surprise, Twilight ignored the apple. Instead, he whickered and touched her hair and then her face with his muzzle.

'Are you OK?' Lauren asked.

Twilight stood still.

'Twilight?' Lauren said, feeling alarmed. 'Is something the matter?'

To her relief, Twilight shook his head.

He could understand Lauren when he was a pony and talk back to her in his own way, but now Lauren wished he

could speak to her properly, with words,
like he did when he was a unicorn. She
wanted to find out why he seemed so
uneasy. 'Are you feeling upset because I
didn't come to see you last night?' she
guessed. 'I'm sorry, but Mum and Dad
had friends over for supper and I fell
asleep before they went to bed. We can
go flying tonight, I promise.'

But her words didn't seem to make
Twilight any happier. He nudged her
with his muzzle again. Lauren frowned.
He was OK, wasn't he?

Of course he is, she thought. She'd asked
him if there was anything wrong and he'd
said no. Pushing her concerns away, she
stroked his tangled mane. Time to get a

move on. He needed a good groom
before Jessica and Mel arrived!

By half past nine, Twilight's grey coat was
spotless, his long tail and mane were
brushed out and his hooves were shining
with hoof oil. But he still seemed restless,
and Lauren couldn't shake off the feeling

that there was something bothering him.

She had just finished tacking him up
when Mel and Jessica rode down the
path on Shadow and Sandy.

Lauren waved. 'Hi!'

'Twilight looks clean,' Jessica
commented.

'Pity about you, Lauren!' Mel grinned.

Lauren looked down at her clothes,
which were very dusty after brushing
Twilight, and grinned back. 'Never mind.
Twilight's the one that matters!'

The three ponies touched noses to say
hello. They were almost as good friends as
Mel, Jessica and Lauren were. Lauren
took hold of the reins and swung herself
into the saddle. 'Let's go!'

They rode down the path into the woods. It was a bright cold morning and the winter sun shone through the treetops, melting the frost on the ground. As soon as the track widened out, the ponies began to pull at their bits.

'I think Sandy wants to canter,' Jessica said, patting the young palomino pony's neck.

'What are we waiting for?' Mel shortened her reins as Shadow tossed his grey head. 'Come on!'

Eventually they reached the clearing. It was a hilly area with lots of bushes and twisty paths leading up and down banks and steep slopes. At first, Lauren, Mel and

Jessica rode cautiously but they soon
grew in confidence and began to try the
banks at a trot and a canter.

'What about that hill?' Mel suggested,
pointing to a high bank that none of
them had ridden down yet.

'No way,' Jessica said. 'It's much too
steep.'

Lauren was standing a little way off
with Twilight. 'What do you think,
Twilight?' Twilight was startled when he
heard his name and Lauren had the
feeling she'd interrupted his thoughts.
'Should we go down it?'

Twilight shook his head. 'We're not
going to do it either,' Lauren called to the
others.

'I've got an idea!' Mel said. 'Let's set a course over the rest of the clearing and then we can time ourselves and see who's the fastest.'

It was great fun but Twilight didn't seem to be as lively as usual. He stumbled several times and once or twice Lauren had to press him on, when normally she had to try and slow him down.

'Are you sure you're all right, Twilight?' she whispered, reining him in.

Twilight nodded but Lauren wasn't convinced. *I'll ask him what's wrong when I turn him into a unicorn tonight,* she decided. *We'll be able to talk properly then.*

CHAPTER

Two

As soon as her parents went to bed that evening, Lauren slipped out of the house. The night air was freezing on her skin and the farm was quiet. Excitement surged through her as she ran down the dark path. Soon she and Twilight would be flying. She could almost feel the wind whipping through her hair, feel the warmth of Twilight's

smooth back. What would they do tonight? Maybe they'd go to the woods and see what animals were around, or maybe jump over the treetops . . .

If Twilight's feeling OK, she reminded herself, thinking how oddly he'd been behaving that day.

'Twilight!' she called softly.

He whinnied.

Lauren reached the gate and quickly spoke the words of the Turning Spell.

'Twilight Star, Twilight Star,
Twinkling high above so far.
Shining light, shining bright,
Will you grant my wish tonight?
Let my little horse forlorn
Be at last a unicorn!'

There was a flash of purple light and
Twilight was transformed from a pony
into a unicorn. His grey coat gleamed
snow-white, his mane and tail hung in
silky strands and in the centre of his

forehead was a sparkling silver horn.

He stepped forward. 'Hello, Lauren.'

His mouth didn't move but Lauren could hear his voice clearly in her head so long as she was touching him or holding a hair from his mane. Nowadays, she made sure that she had one of his hairs with her at all times in case she needed to turn him into a unicorn and speak to him. 'Are you all right?' she asked, stroking his forelock.

'I'm fine,' Twilight said, but he let out a long sigh.

Lauren wondered why he seemed so down. *Maybe if we go flying it will cheer him up.* 'Do you want to go flying?' she suggested.

Twilight shook his head. 'No. I don't feel like it.'

Lauren was astonished. 'Why not?' The only time she'd ever known Twilight turn down the chance to go flying had been when he had been ill.

'I feel really tired after all the cantering and jumping today,' Twilight replied.

'OK,' Lauren said slowly. 'I suppose we can always go tomorrow instead.' She put her arms round his neck, feeling confused. It was not like Twilight to refuse a chance to go flying.

Another long sad sigh trembled through him.

'Twilight, what is it?' Lauren said, stepping back and looking at him.

'Something's wrong, I know it is. Are you ill? Maybe I should get the vet?'

'No,' Twilight said. 'I don't feel ill. I'm . . . tired.' He saw her concerned expression. 'I really don't feel ill. I'd tell you if I did, I promise. I think I just need to rest. Will you turn me back into a pony, please?'

Lauren stroked him worriedly. Twilight wasn't behaving like himself at all. But what could she do? 'OK,' she said and, giving him a kiss, she said the Undoing Spell.

'Good night,' she murmured as the purple flash faded and Twilight looked like an ordinary pony once again.

Twilight whickered softly and Lauren headed back towards the house, hoping he'd feel better in the morning.

★

Lauren got up early the next day to
check on Twilight. To her relief he
whinnied cheerfully when he saw her.

'Are you feeling better?' she asked.

Twilight nodded.

He definitely seemed livelier. He was
holding his head high and his eyes had
lost their worried look. Lauren felt

relieved. Perhaps he *had* just been tired the night before.

'We can go out for a ride later,' she told him.

After they had both had breakfast and Lauren had groomed Twilight, she tacked him up and rode into the woods. She decided to ride to the clearing with the banks and hills again. It was different riding there on her own, instead of with Mel and Jessica, but Lauren didn't mind. It was another crisp cold morning and it was great to be with Twilight, trotting along the frosty tracks. Everything was quiet, still and peaceful.

When they reached the clearing, Lauren saw that there were two other riders already there. The girls looked a few years older than her – maybe twelve or thirteen. They were cantering down the banks on their ponies, shouting to each other. Lauren halted, not sure if she should join in.

'Perhaps we should go back,' she murmured to Twilight. But then one of the girls' horses – a pretty bay Arab with four white socks – noticed them. She lifted her head and whinnied. Both girls looked round.

'Hi there!' called the girl on the bay mare. She had blonde hair tied in a short stubby ponytail under her riding hat.

'Hi,' Lauren said shyly.

'Were you coming to ride here?' the

girl asked, riding over.

Lauren nodded. 'But it doesn't matter. I can come back another day.'

'No, it's OK,' the girl said. 'We don't mind. There's room for all of us. My name's Jo-Ann, by the way. And this is my pony, Beauty.'

Lauren looked at the pretty bay mare with her dished face and large dark eyes. 'She is beautiful.'

'Thanks,' Jo-Ann smiled. 'So, what's your name?'

'Lauren. And this is Twilight.'

The other girl came over. 'I'm Grace,' she said. 'And this is Windfall,' she added, patting the neck of her chestnut pony.

'Do you want to ride with us?' asked Jo-Ann.

'OK,' Lauren agreed. She and Twilight set off after the others. He was smaller than the other two ponies but he kept up well, twisting and turning and cantering sure-footedly down the banks. Jo-Ann was a very daring rider. After cantering up and down the hills, she started to jump any bushes or fallen logs she could find – even logs that had spiky branches sticking up and that were lying on uneven ground. She didn't seem to worry about safety. Lauren and Grace stopped to watch her.

Lauren gasped as Beauty only just managed to clear a huge tree trunk.

'That was close!' Jo-Ann grinned, pulling Beauty up and patting her. She looked around. 'What shall I do next?' Her eyes fell on the very steep bank. 'I know! How about I try that bank over there?'

'No way!' Grace said. 'It's much too steep and it might be slippery.'

'I bet Beauty could manage it,' Jo-Ann said thoughtfully.

'Don't do it,' Grace advised. 'These

guys have done enough.' She patted
Windfall's warm neck. 'Come on, let's
take them home.'

'I guess they are quite hot,' Jo-Ann
agreed reluctantly. 'Let's walk back to cool
them off.' She turned to Lauren. 'Nice to
meet you, Lauren. See you around.'

'Yeah, bye!' Lauren called.

She waved as the older girls rode off,
and then stroked Twilight's mane. 'Come
on, let's go home too.' She didn't want to
tire him out again. She was looking
forward to flying that night!

As they reached the farm, Lauren saw
Max and Buddy heading out along the
drive. Max had his skateboard with him.

'Are you going round to Leo and
Steven's?' she asked.

Max nodded. 'Yeah, Leo's got a new
skateboard and he said I could try it, then
we're going to take Buddy for a walk.'

Buddy wagged his plumy tail and
woofed. He might not be able to
understand humans in the way that
Twilight could but he could certainly
understand the words *Buddy* and *walk*!

'You'll like that, won't you, boy?' Max
said, giving Buddy a hug. 'You like Leo
and Steven.' Buddy licked his face in
reply and Max giggled.

Lauren grinned. It was great seeing
Max and Buddy so happy together. When
Max had first made friends with their

neighbours, Steven and Leo Vance, he had
neglected Buddy a bit, but then he had
found out his new friends liked dogs as
much as he did and now Buddy always
went with him when he went to their
house.

'See you later, Lauren,' Max said, setting
off again.

'Later,' Lauren replied and she rode
Twilight back to his stable.

After she had untacked him and

washed him down, she turned him out into the field. 'I'll come out this evening and we can go flying. OK?'

Twilight didn't respond.

'Twilight?' Lauren said.

He whickered quietly. *Tonight*, Lauren thought and, giving him a hug, she went in for lunch.

That night, Twilight was waiting for Lauren by the gate. He seemed tense again; he was pacing up and down and his head was held high. Lauren quickly turned him into a unicorn. 'Hi, boy. Are you ready to go flying then?'

Twilight shook his head.

'Why not?' Lauren demanded. 'We

didn't do that much today!'

Twilight interrupted her. 'It's not because I'm tired.'

'So, why can't we go flying then?'

Twilight pawed the ground unhappily. 'Because . . . because I can't.'

Lauren didn't understand. 'What do you mean, you can't?' She touched his neck in concern. 'Are you ill or something?'

'No. I can't go flying because . . .' Twilight took a deep breath and looked miserably at her. 'Because my magic powers have stopped working!'

CHAPTER

Three

Lauren stared. 'What do you mean, your powers have stopped working? For how long?'

Twilight looked at the ground. 'Forever.'

Lauren felt as if a bucket of ice had just been tipped all over her. 'Forever!' she echoed.

Twilight nodded. 'It happens

sometimes,' he said, not meeting her eyes.
'Unicorns lose their powers. Their magic
just fades and goes away. It means I can't
do any magic any more – I can't look
into the seeing stones; I can't heal
wounds; I can't make people feel braver. I
can't do any of those things.'

Lauren's mind seemed to spin. 'And
you can't fly?'

'No.'

Lauren was struck by an awful thought.
'But you'll always be able to turn into a
unicorn, won't you? I'll always be able to
speak to you like this?'

'I don't know.' Twilight hesitated.
'Probably not,' he added in a very small
voice. 'My powers will probably all

disappear in the end.'

Lauren's stomach plunged. She didn't know what to say.

'I . . . I suppose this means you won't love me any more,' Twilight said.

'What?' Lauren frowned. 'Of course I'll love you.'

Twilight looked taken aback. 'But . . . but I won't be able to do magic. I'll just be an ordinary pony.'

'As if that matters!' Lauren burst out.

She was astonished that he could think
this would change the way she felt about
him. 'Twilight, you're my best friend.' She
hugged him fiercely. 'How *could* you
think that losing your powers would
change that? I loved you before I knew
you were a unicorn, remember? It doesn't
matter to me whether you're magical or
not.'

'So, you won't want me to go away?'
Twilight spoke very slowly. 'You won't
want to get rid of me?'

'Get rid of you? No way!'

A look of confusion crossed Twilight's
face. 'But . . . but I thought . . .' He
looked even more upset than before.

'I can't believe you'd think that I'd

want to get rid of you!' Lauren exclaimed. 'All that matters, Twilight, is that we're together.'

Twilight scraped his foot on the ground. 'Oh,' he said in a very small voice.

Feeling utterly bewildered, Lauren put her arms round him. What was going on? A hard lump of tears blocked her throat. But she tried not to cry. Twilight was obviously very upset. She'd only make him more miserable if she started crying.

'Maybe I'd better turn you back into a pony,' she said, her voice coming out in a whisper.

Twilight nodded sadly.

Lauren said the words of the Undoing Spell and Twilight turned back into a pony.

''Night, Twilight,' she whispered.

He whickered unhappily as she walked slowly back to the house.

When she got back to her bedroom, she sat down on the bed. Twilight's magic was fading! She undressed and got into bed. She couldn't believe it. No more magic. No more flying. And, maybe soon, no more talking to her best friend. But the worst thing of all was how unhappy this was making Twilight. Did he really think she wouldn't love him any more, just because he wasn't a unicorn?

⋆

Lauren lay awake for ages that night and when she woke up, her first thought was that she'd had a bad dream. She blinked, and realized it hadn't been a dream at all. It was real. Twilight was losing his magic powers.

She pulled on her clothes and went downstairs. Her mum, dad and Max were in the kitchen.

'Morning, sleepyhead!' her dad teased.

Not wanting her parents to see how tired she felt in case they wanted to know why, Lauren forced a smile. 'Morning.'

Mrs Foster was making a pot of coffee. 'We almost sent Buddy in to wake you up. Twilight will be wondering where his breakfast is.'

'I'll go and feed him now,' Lauren said,
glad of an excuse to get out of the house.

Buddy trotted over to her and pushed
his body between her legs. Lauren made
a fuss of him to try and hide her sadness
from her family. When she sat down to
pull her boots on, Buddy plonked his
head on her lap and looked up at her
with big brown eyes. It was as if he could
sense there was something wrong.

'Good boy,' Lauren whispered, blinking hard.

'What time are you going over to Leo and Steven's, Max?' Mrs Foster asked.

Max scraped the last of his cereal bowl clean. 'Half past nine. I can't wait! They got their new puppy last night.'

Lauren had forgotten that Steven and Leo were getting their new puppy that weekend.

'Have they decided what they're going to call her?' asked Mrs Foster.

Max grinned. 'Buggy!'

'Buggy?' Mrs Foster echoed doubtfully.

'It's short for Love Bug; that's what Steven and Leo's mum said the puppy's proper name is.'

Mr Foster shook his head. 'Buddy and Buggy. That's going to be a bit confusing!'

'I think Buggy's a cool name. She and Buddy are going to be best friends!' Max said happily. 'I can't wait to see her.'

Mrs Foster smiled. 'I'm with you there. In fact, I think I might just have to walk round with you when you go to their house this morning.' She glanced at Lauren. 'Do you want to come too, Lauren?'

Knowing that her mum would think it was strange if she said no, Lauren nodded. 'Yes, please.' She stood up and went to the door. First she had to feed Twilight. As she walked down to his field, she felt odd. She wasn't quite sure how to act. What would she say to him?

Twilight was standing by the gate looking very miserable. His head was low and his eyes seemed to have lost their sparkle.

'Hey, boy,' Lauren said.

He nuzzled her gently. Neither of them met the other's eyes.

Lauren fetched Twilight his breakfast but he hardly touched it. He nibbled a few flakes of the coarse mix and then left the rest.

Lauren stroked him. 'Not feeling hungry today?'

Twilight shook his head.

'Me neither,' Lauren told him. Just looking at how sad Twilight was made her eyes prickle with tears.

But he'll still be my pony, she reminded herself. *I'll still be able to see him and ride him every day. And the more fuss I make of him, the more he might believe that I do still love him.*

Feeling a bit better, she started on the stable chores – cleaning out and refilling Twilight's water buckets, brushing the concrete in front of the stables and tidying the tack room. After a while, she heard her mum calling.

'Lauren! We're going to Steven and Leo's now!'

'Coming!' Lauren called back.

She went over to where Twilight was standing unhappily by the gate and rubbed his neck. 'I'll be back soon,' she promised, giving him a kiss.

Buggy was the cutest puppy ever! She was a flat-coated retriever with a soft, jet-black coat, bright sparkling eyes, big paws and a tail that never seemed to stop wagging. As Lauren and Max and Mrs Foster crowded round, the puppy wriggled in Leo's arms, trying to lick everyone's faces and hands with her pink tongue. Buddy pressed forward and Buggy licked him on the nose.

'Can I put her on the grass, Mum?' Leo begged.

'Yeah,' Steven said. 'Let's see how she likes Buddy.'

Their mum, Helen, nodded. 'All right.'

As soon as Buggy was on the floor, she bounded over to Buddy, her tail going round and round like a propeller. She was only as high as his tummy but she didn't seem scared at all. She leapt on Buddy, licking his mouth and pulling at his ears.

Buddy's tail started to wag and he crouched down to look at her more closely.

The puppy yapped at him and he woofed back in a deep voice. Then he lay down and let her jump all over him, rolling over on his back so she could scrabble on to his tummy.

After a few minutes they jumped up

and began to chase each other around the garden.

'Looks like they're going to be friends,' Helen smiled.

Leo turned to Max. 'When Buggy gets bigger we'll be able to take them on walks together.'

'And she can run round the skateboard course like Buddy does,' said Steven.

'We can have races!' Leo added.

Max nodded eagerly. 'It'll be cool!'

Lauren smiled. Max was going to have loads of fun taking Buddy to play with Leo, Steven and Buggy. She knew that having friends with pets was great fun. She loved riding with Mel and Jessica.

And I'll still be able to do that when Twilight's magic is gone, she reflected. She thought of Twilight's sad face that morning and suddenly wanted to get back to him. She had to make him realize that it didn't matter if he lost his magic.

'Is it OK if I go back now, Mum?' she asked.

'Of course,' replied Mrs Foster. 'I'll see you later.'

Lauren hurried home. Twilight was standing by the gate where she had left him, not looking any happier. Climbing over it, Lauren put an arm round his neck and leant her cheek against his neck. 'Oh, Twilight,' she whispered. 'Losing your powers must be horrible for you but it's going to be OK, I promise. We'll still be able to have lots of fun together.'

She'd hoped her words might cheer Twilight up but he still looked miserable.

Lauren wracked her brains to think of something she could do to make him feel better. Maybe if they went out for a ride in the woods it would help him realize how much fun they could have, even if he was just a pony.

'How about we go for a ride?' she suggested. 'We could go to the place with the banks and hills again.'

Twilight gave a tiny nod.

Lauren kissed him. 'OK. I'll go and ring Mel and Jessica and see if they want to come too.'

Four

Jessica couldn't come out for a ride because she was going into town with her stepsister, Samantha, but Mel was keen to go to the woods again.

She came over at eleven. 'So, did you go to the clearing yesterday?' she asked as they rode down the track, away from the farm.

'Yes,' Lauren replied. 'There were two girls there. They let me ride with them.' She patted Twilight. 'We had fun, didn't we, boy?' He snorted quietly. Lauren crossed her fingers. She desperately wanted him to see what a good time they could have without magic.

As they reached the clearing they heard voices.

'That might be those girls,' Lauren said.

She and Mel rode into the clearing. Sure enough, Jo-Ann and Grace were there on Beauty and Windfall. They had set up jumps at the bottom of some of the banks.

'Hi, Lauren!' Jo-Ann called, waving. She looked again. 'Mel!' she exclaimed.

'Hello.'

'Hi, Jo-Ann,' Mel called.

'Do you two know each other?' Lauren asked in surprise.

Mel nodded as Jo-Ann rode over to them. 'Our mums are friends,' she explained. She smiled at Jo-Ann. 'Is this your new pony? Mum told me you'd just got one.'

'Yes, this is Beauty,' Jo-Ann replied. The

pretty bay tossed her head. 'She's brilliant. She's really fast and loves jumping. Is Shadow still jumping OK?'

Mel nodded. 'Ever since last summer he's been fine.'

Lauren stroked Twilight's neck to hide a smile. When she had first met Mel, Shadow had been scared of jumping but she and Twilight had helped him get over his fear. It had been one of the first things they had done together after Lauren had found out Twilight was a unicorn. He had been able to use his magic powers to fill Shadow with courage – enough to leap out of his barn when it was on fire! She wondered if he was remembering it too.

I suppose we won't be helping any more people now. Lauren pushed the thought away. This wasn't the time to feel sorry for herself. Twilight needed her to be cheerful.

'Can we have a go at the jumps?' she asked Jo-Ann.

'Sure,' Jo-Ann replied.

'Come on!' Grace called.

Soon, Lauren and Mel were cantering

down the banks and over the jumps with
the two older girls. Mel only did the
lower jumps but Lauren tried some of
the bigger ones. Not all of them, though.
Jo-Ann had made a few massive jumps
out of logs and old branches.

'I don't know how you dare do that!'
Mel called as Jo-Ann rode down a
particularly steep bank with a huge brush
jump at the bottom.

'It's fun!' Jo-Ann laughed, pulling
Beauty to a halt. The pony snorted and
pulled at her bit.

'Why don't you have a go?' Jo-Ann
urged Lauren and Mel.

Mel shook her head. 'It's way too big
for Shadow and me.'

Jo-Ann turned to Lauren. 'How about you, Lauren? Twilight seems really good at jumping.'

Lauren hesitated. Part of her longed to canter down the bank and fly over the jump, but then she looked at the steep uneven surface and shook her head. Jo-Ann might have managed it fine but it did look tricky. She'd never forgive herself if Twilight hurt himself. 'No, I don't think I will,' she said.

Jo-Ann looked teasingly at her. 'Chicken!'

'Jo-Ann!' Grace protested. 'Don't hassle Lauren. If she doesn't want to do it, she doesn't have to.'

'Sorry.' Jo-Ann shrugged. 'Looks like I'll

have to do it on my own, then.' She cantered towards the bank and sped down it. Beauty cleared the jump easily.

Jo-Ann patted her and headed towards the really steep bank that no one had dared to go down yet.

'Be careful, Jo!' Grace warned.

'Stop fussing,' Jo-Ann replied. 'Beauty will manage it fine.'

The other three watched as she headed towards it. Beauty sped up, fighting for her head. Jo-Ann circled her, got her steady and then tried again. It was so steep that Beauty had to tuck her hocks right underneath her. Lauren gasped as the bank crumbled a little and Beauty slid a few metres, but Jo-Ann sat very still and

let her find her footing again. In a couple
more strides, they safely reached the
bottom of the bank.

'Good girl!' Jo-Ann praised.

'Cool!' Mel said.

Grace nodded. 'That was great riding,
Jo.'

'She's a great pony!' Jo-Ann said,
patting the mare. She looked at the bank.
'Maybe I could put a jump at the
bottom.'

Grace shook her head. 'It's hard enough to get down without a jump there.'

'I suppose,' Jo-Ann replied, not sounding convinced.

'Come on,' Grace said. 'Why don't we take the ponies to the creek for a drink?'

'All right.' Jo-Ann turned to Lauren and Mel. 'Are you going to come as well?'

They nodded and the four of them set off through the trees. As they rode, Lauren learned that Grace and Jo-Ann kept their ponies at a livery stables that Grace's mum owned. It was fun hearing about the ponies there, and about all the shows that Grace and Jo-Ann competed in. Lauren hoped Twilight was enjoying himself too.

It doesn't matter one bit that he can't be a unicorn, she told herself. *We'll still be able to go for rides like this and do all sorts of things. After all, Mel and Jessica love Shadow and Sandy and they aren't unicorns.*

Lauren frowned as she realized she'd been so shocked by the news the night before that she hadn't asked Twilight why unicorns lost their powers at all, or if there was any way of stopping it. Perhaps there was some way of getting his powers back! Hope flickered through her. If there was anything – anything at all – she could do, then she would give it a try to make him happy again.

I'll ask him tonight, she thought. Then

another idea struck her. What about her unicorn book? It had lots of information about unicorns in it. Maybe one of the chapters would explain how they could stop Twilight's magic from fading.

I'll look at it when I get home, she decided.

As soon as Lauren untacked Twilight after their ride, she ran into the house and found her precious book. *The Life of a Unicorn* was a very old book with a faded blue cover. Mrs Fontana, who owned the bookshop in town, had given it to Lauren when she had first got Twilight. Mrs Fontana was one of the few people who knew about Twilight, because she had once owned a unicorn herself.

Lauren began to leaf through the yellowing pages. There were chapters on unicorn myths, unicorn habits, and all sorts of information about Arcadia, the magic land that the unicorns came from.

Lauren flicked through chapter after chapter. There had to be something about unicorns losing their powers!

She stopped at the end of the book. There was nothing. Not a single mention of a unicorn's magic fading.

Weird, Lauren thought. *Twilight made it sound like it happened quite often. It's odd the book doesn't say anything about it at all.*

She frowned. She'd have to question him more that night.

★

'Twilight, I looked in the unicorn book and it didn't say anything about unicorns losing their powers,' Lauren said as soon as she had turned Twilight into a unicorn.

'Well, it does happen,' Twilight said quickly.

'Is there anything that can be done to stop it or to bring them back?' Lauren asked.

'No,' he muttered, scraping at the ground with his front hoof. 'I don't think so.'

'Maybe if you tell me everything you know about it, we can think of something to try,' Lauren urged him.

Twilight looked uncomfortable. 'I can't

remember much.'

Lauren frowned. 'How can we find out more?' Her eyes widened. 'Of course!' she exclaimed. 'Mrs Fontana! She knows lots about unicorns – we can ask her.'

Twilight shook his head. 'I'm sure she won't be able to help, Lauren . . .'

But Lauren refused to give up hope. 'It's worth asking her,' she interrupted. Mrs Fontana always seemed to know what to do when there was a problem with Twilight. 'I'll see if Mum will drive me to her shop in the morning.' She hugged Twilight. 'Don't worry, Mrs Fontana will be able to help us, I'm sure!'

Twilight snorted unhappily. Lauren couldn't understand why he didn't look

convinced. After all, if he was so
depressed about losing his magic powers,
surely he'd try anything to get them
back?

CHAPTER

Five

Deep in the heart of Arcadia, the three Unicorn Elders stood by the stone table, their golden, silver and bronze horns sparkling in the moonlight. The picture that had been there moments before had vanished and all that was left of the magic was a wisp of purple smoke drifting across the table.

'Twilight is very unhappy,' Ira, the

unicorn with the golden horn, said heavily.

'He is so young,' sighed Rohan, the bronze-horned unicorn. 'And he loves Lauren very much.'

Sidra lifted her head, her silver horn flashing in the starlight. 'Yes, but this is how it has to be.' She pricked up her ears. 'He must see that this is for the best – that it is an honour to be chosen. Maybe I should visit him again and talk to him some more.'

'Yes,' the other two unicorns agreed.

'Will you go tomorrow night?' Ira asked.

Sidra nodded. 'I will.'

★

'Is there something in particular you want from the bookshop?' Mrs Foster asked as she drove Lauren into town the next morning. It was a very cold day and the sky was turning a snowy white.

'I just want a new book to read,' Lauren replied casually. 'I've got the money that Auntie Hilary sent to me, and I thought I might spend it on a book.'

Mrs Foster nodded. 'Any idea what book you'd like?'

'Not yet,' Lauren said. 'Is it OK if I spend some time browsing?'

'Well, it looks like it's going to snow, so we'd better not be too long,' her mum replied. 'I'll leave you at Mrs Fontana's while I do the rest of my shopping.'

'Thanks,' Lauren said, feeling relieved. Hopefully she'd get to spend some time with Mrs Fontana on her own. She stared out of the window at the houses flashing by and, as soft snowflakes began to fall, she wondered what Mrs Fontana would say.

Mrs Fontana's bookshop never seemed to change. There were always piles of books on the floor and the air always smelt

slightly of blackcurrants. Lauren thought
it was the smell of magic even though
her mum said it was the fruit tea that Mrs
Fontana drank. The elderly lady was
standing at the counter with her grey
hair tied back in a bun and her soft
yellow shawl wrapped round her
shoulders. She was talking to Walter, her

little black and white terrier dog.

'Hello, Lauren,' she said, looking up as Lauren entered. 'How are you?'

'Fine, thank you,' Lauren replied. She glanced around to check that there was no one else in the shop.

'We're alone,' Mrs Fontana said, as if she could read Lauren's thoughts. She frowned. 'Are you all right, my dear? You look worried.'

The words burst out of Lauren. 'Oh, Mrs Fontana, I really need your help. Twilight's losing his magic powers!'

Mrs Fontana looked astonished. 'What?'

Lauren quickly told her everything. 'He said that it happens to unicorns sometimes but I can't find any mention of it in the book and I want to know if there's anything we can do. It's making him so unhappy!' She looked pleadingly at Mrs Fontana. 'Do you know if there's anything that will stop his magic from fading?'

Mrs Fontana looked puzzled. 'I'm sorry, Lauren, but I don't know what to say. I've never heard of a unicorn losing its powers before – not permanently, anyway. Are you sure that's what Twilight said was happening?'

'Positive,' Lauren replied. 'He said it often happens and that there's nothing we can do.'

'How strange.' Mrs Fontana rubbed her forehead. 'Why don't you tell me exactly what happened?'

Lauren sat on a long-legged stool and rested her chin on her hands. 'He was fine one day, and the next he seemed really miserable. At first he said he was just tired but then he told me about his magic fading. He's so unhappy! I've tried telling him that I'll still love him even if he's just a regular pony but it doesn't seem to have helped.' She bit her lip. 'It's awful seeing him like this, Mrs Fontana! If there's anything I can do, I want to do it.'

'I'm sure you do, Lauren.' Mrs Fontana hesitated. 'But you know, I think there's something else going on and Twilight's not telling you everything. Unicorns don't lose their powers permanently. It just doesn't happen.'

Lauren's heart leapt. 'Really?'

Mrs Fontana nodded.

'So why have Twilight's powers gone?' Lauren asked. 'Why can't he fly any more?'

'I don't know,' Mrs Fontana admitted. 'I can only assume that there's something Twilight hasn't told you about. My advice is to try and get him to talk to you. But don't push him too hard,' she warned. 'He might clam up even more.'

'OK,' Lauren agreed. Her head was whirling. It felt odd to think that there was something Twilight wasn't telling her. 'I just don't understand why he

would keep something secret. I'm his
best friend – he should be able to tell me
anything!'

'Oh, Lauren, people keep secrets for all
sorts of reasons,' Mrs Fontana replied.
'Twilight is probably doing what he
thinks is best. Just let him know that
you'll listen when he's ready to talk.' She
squeezed Lauren's hand. 'He might be
your unicorn, Lauren, but he's also your
friend. Treat him like you would any of
your other friends if you thought they
had a problem. He'll tell you what's going
on in his own good time.'

Just then the doorbell tinkled and a
man came in with a little boy. Walter
trotted over to say hello, and Lauren

knew her conversation with Mrs Fontana
was over.

'Thanks, Mrs Fontana,' she said.

'Good luck!' Mrs Fontana smiled. 'And
now, you'd better choose a book before
your mum gets back and wonders what
you've been doing all this time.'

Lauren thought about what Mrs Fontana
had said all day. She felt better knowing
that Mrs Fontana had never heard of a
unicorn's magic fading away permanently
before. She just wished she knew exactly
what was going on.

'Are you sure there's nothing else you
want to tell me?' Lauren said to Twilight
as she stroked his silky mane that night.

'No,' he sighed.

'Really sure?' Lauren persisted.

'Yes. Can we talk about something else?'

Lauren bit her lip with frustration. She remembered what Mrs Fontana had said about letting Twilight talk to her in his own time, so she just nodded. 'Sure. But you can tell me anything, Twilight, you know that. Anything at all.'

He stared miserably at the ground. Lauren couldn't bear seeing him look so sad.

'I know, how about I go and get you some carrots from the tack room as a treat? Dad put a new sack in there this afternoon.'

Twilight nodded and she hurried away.

When she came back with the carrots, Twilight was shaking his head. 'I've got to tell her!' he was muttering. 'I can't do this.'

Lauren froze. What was he talking about?

'I just can't!' Twilight said to himself.

'Twilight?' Lauren whispered.

Twilight looked round, startled. 'Lauren! I didn't see you there.'

'What were you talking about?' she asked, hurrying over. 'What have you got to tell me?'

'Nothing. I . . . I wasn't talking about you,' Twilight said quickly.

Lauren felt her temper flare. She knew

that wasn't true. 'Twilight!' she exclaimed
angrily. 'Just . . .' She broke off, recalling
what Mrs Fontana had said about not
putting pressure on him in case he
clammed up even more. 'OK,' she said,
trying to stay calm. 'If you don't want to
talk about it, that's fine.'

Twilight relaxed slightly and as she fed
him a carrot, she changed the subject. 'It
was fun yesterday, wasn't it? Riding with
Jo-Ann and Grace, I mean. Do you like
Beauty and Windfall?'

Twilight nodded. 'Yes, and I liked
cantering up and down the banks too.'

'We'll have to go again,' Lauren said.
'And go on some more fun rides and
wander by the creek. There are so many

things we can do, especially when summer comes,' she went on, trying to remind him that they could have fun whether he was a unicorn or not. 'Maybe we could even go camping!'

'Maybe,' Twilight said in a quiet voice.

Lauren stayed with him for an hour, talking about all the great things they could do together, before she went inside. She sat down on her bed, feeling frustrated. However nice it was talking to Twilight, she still hadn't found out what was going on.

Getting undressed, she climbed into bed and pulled her duvet over her. But she couldn't sleep. She and Twilight were best friends. They shouldn't keep secrets

from each other. *I wouldn't keep a secret from him*, she thought.

She hesitated and then pushed her duvet back. She couldn't go on like this. Mrs Fontana might have said to take it gently but she *had* to know what was going on. Getting out of bed, she pulled her clothes back on. Then she crept downstairs and hurried outside. She would beg Twilight to tell her what the matter was, make him see that whatever it was, they could overcome it together.

Feeling fired up with determination, she ran down the path to his field. Suddenly she stopped dead.

'Twilight!' she whispered in astonishment.

Twilight was standing in his field, but he wasn't a pony, like she had left him. His coat was gleaming silvery-white and his horn was glittering. He was a unicorn!

And that wasn't all. Standing beside him was another unicorn! It had its head bent and was talking urgently to Twilight. Lauren stared in shock. This unicorn was bigger than Twilight, with a coat that sparkled like freshly fallen snow. It had a long silver horn, glittering dark eyes and a face so beautiful that just looking at it made Lauren hold her breath.

The unicorn whinnied and flew into the air without noticing Lauren.

Stunned, Lauren watched Twilight plunge upwards too, and side by side the two unicorns cantered away into the starry sky.

CHAPTER
Six

Lauren took a step forward and stared at the empty sky. Twilight had said he couldn't fly any more. He had told her that his powers had gone. How *could* he have just flown away?

There was only one answer. Twilight had been lying to her!

Lauren shook her head in disbelief. She couldn't believe that all the time, when

she'd been so worried about him, he
hadn't lost his powers at all.

Turning, she ran back to the house.

When she reached her bedroom she
threw herself down on her bed. The
unicorn book slipped on to the floor and
landed with a thud. It fell awkwardly, half
open, with its beautiful old pages bent
and creased. Lauren automatically reached
down to pick it up. As she did, she
noticed that it had fallen open at a
picture. Icy fingers ran down her spine. It
showed two unicorns cantering into the
sky – one big, one small, exactly like
Twilight and the unicorn she'd seen just
now.

With her heart thudding painfully,

Lauren pulled the book closer and read
the title below the picture:

A Unicorn Elder taking a Chosen
Unicorn back to Arcadia.

Not understanding, Lauren scanned the
rest of the words.

Pony unicorns who prove themselves to be

particularly brave and resourceful in the human world will often be chosen to return to Arcadia. There they will train to be assistants to the Unicorn Elders, helping the Elders to rule Arcadia and watch over the human world. It is a great honour to be chosen and, in time, these chosen unicorns will one day become Unicorn Elders themselves. A chosen unicorn will be visited by a Unicorn Elder several times before the *unicorn has to say goodbye to his or her human friend and leave the human world forever.*

Leave the human world forever. The words echoed around in Lauren's head. Twilight must have been chosen to go to Arcadia! Was that where he'd been going with the other unicorn tonight?

Did that mean she was never going to see him again?

Jumping off her bed, Lauren raced to her window.

Twilight was in his field, grazing peacefully. For one wild moment Lauren wondered if she'd just imagined the sight of him flying into the sky with another unicorn. Maybe it was all a dream? But it wasn't. She'd seen both unicorns flying away as clearly as she saw Twilight in his field now.

She sank down on to the window seat. The Unicorn Elder must have been visiting Twilight that night. But maybe the *next* time . . .

'No,' Lauren whispered out loud. 'He can't go to Arcadia.'

But the more she thought about it, the more it all made sense. That first morning when he'd been so quiet – well, that must have been after the first visit from the Unicorn Elder, after Twilight had been told he'd been chosen. And the reason he had looked so sad even when Lauren had

said she didn't mind if he lost his powers
must have been because he'd known that
they wouldn't be together much longer.

Why didn't he tell me? Lauren thought
desperately. *He must have known he was
going to have to tell me some time. Unless . . .*

Her stomach flipped over.

Perhaps Twilight hadn't been planning
to tell her at all. Perhaps he'd been
intending just to vanish one night.

Twilight wouldn't do that, she told
herself, but why else would Twilight have
kept his news secret? Why else would he
have lied to her?

Lauren began to tremble. Moving like a
robot, she took off her clothes and pulled
on her pyjamas, then crawled under the

duvet. She couldn't stop shivering. She felt utterly betrayed by her best friend. How could he have thought of leaving without telling her? How could he have thought of leaving at all?

Oh, Twilight, she cried silently in her head. *I could never leave you.*

Pulling the duvet over her head, a sob choked through her and soon her pillow was soaked with tears.

The next morning, Lauren stayed in bed until she heard her mum getting up. For the first time ever, she didn't want to go out to Twilight's field. But when she heard her mum waking Max up, she knew she couldn't stay in bed much longer. She had to get up now to avoid facing her mum and Max in the kitchen. They would see at once that she'd been crying. Putting on her crumpled jeans, she hurried outside before they came downstairs.

Twilight was waiting by his gate. To

Lauren's surprise, he lifted his head and whinnied happily. When she reached the gate he nuzzled her as if they were best friends again.

Her heart sank with misery. She knew why he was happy this morning. It was because he'd spent the night before talking to the other unicorn, and planning his return to Arcadia.

She pushed him away. 'I'll get your breakfast,' she said, barely able to stop her voice shaking with hurt. Ignoring his look of surprise, she walked away.

When she returned with his coarse mix, Twilight whinnied.

'Here,' she said abruptly, putting the bucket down.

Twilight nudged her but she stepped back. 'No, don't do that!' she exclaimed.

Twilight took a mouthful and then, looking at her cheekily from under his forelock, he snorted the food into the air. Normally when he messed around, it made Lauren smile. But right then, her heart felt like a stone in her chest. How could he be so cheerful when he knew

he was leaving her forever?

She guessed that whatever the other unicorn had said to him the night before had made Twilight realize that his decision to leave was the right one.

Her throat ached. Turning round, she hurried away before he could see the tears in her eyes.

Twilight whickered but she ignored him and carried on. She forced herself not to turn round even though he whinnied again and again. He was still whinnying when she reached the house and went inside, slamming the door behind her.

After breakfast, Lauren went to her room.

To avoid going outside she decided to tidy her room. She had just taken all the books off the shelves above her bed when Mel rang.

'Hi!' Mel said cheerfully. 'Shall we go for a ride today? There isn't much snow – we could go to the clearing again.'

'Um . . . no thanks.' Lauren didn't feel like doing anything with Twilight.

'Why not?' Mel said in surprise.

'I don't feel very well,' Lauren lied.

'What's the matter?' asked Mel.

Lauren thought quickly. 'I've got a cold. My throat's really sore. I'd better not talk for long.'

'Oh, OK. Well, I hope you feel better soon,' Mel told her. 'I'll give you a ring tonight. Maybe we could go for a ride tomorrow?'

'Maybe,' Lauren whispered. Saying goodbye, she put the phone down.

She walked over to the window and stared out. Twilight was standing by the gate with his ears pricked up hopefully. He looked like he was waiting for her. How could he not realize how much he was hurting her?

Wrapping her arms round herself, Lauren tried to imagine life without him. No unicorn, no pony, no best friend.

As if sensing that she was watching, Twilight looked up at the window. Swallowing her tears, Lauren quickly turned away.

CHAPTER
Seven

As Lauren fed Twilight that evening and refilled his water buckets, he nudged her again and again. Lauren guessed he was trying to tell her that he wanted to be turned into a unicorn.

'I'm not going to come out later,' she muttered. 'I'll see you in the morning, Twilight.' *If you're still here*.

Twilight whickered urgently but

Lauren shook her head.

Her heart aching, she trudged back to the house.

She was just pulling her boots off when the phone rang. It was Jessica. 'Hi. How are you feeling?'

'Fine,' Lauren said, before remembering she was supposed to be ill. 'My throat's still a bit sore though,' she added hastily.

'Mel said you weren't well. She's here now – she's staying the night.'

'Hi, Lauren!' Lauren heard Mel shout in the background.

'Are you going to be OK to ride tomorrow?' Jessica asked.

'I'm not sure,' Lauren said. 'I don't think so.'

'Is everything all right?' said Jessica. 'You sound really down.'

'I'm OK,' Lauren told her.

Mel took the phone from Jessica. 'Are you still feeling ill?'

'Yes.' Lauren quickly changed the subject. 'How was the ride today?'

'Fun,' Mel answered. 'We went to the clearing again after lunch. Jo-Ann and Grace weren't there this time.'

Lauren could hear Twilight
whinnying but she ignored
him. 'Jo-Ann had a riding
lesson today and was going
to go to the clearing later
this afternoon,' Lauren
remembered.

'Yes, that's right,' said
Mel. 'She must have got
there after us. I wonder if
she tried that bank again.
She's so brave!'

'Yeah,' Lauren said.

'Well, I'd better go,' Mel told her. 'I'll
ring you tomorrow. Get better soon! Jess
and I want to go on as many rides as we
can before it gets really snowy but we

don't want to go without you.'

Lauren hung up the phone and sat down. When Twilight left she wouldn't be able to go riding with Mel and Jessica any more. Slowly, her unhappiness turned to anger. *I'll get another pony*, she thought. *I don't need Twilight. I don't need him at all.*

She stood up and started laying the table for supper. Max was staying at Steven and Leo's house that night so it was just her and her mum and dad. She had just finished setting three places when the phone rang again.

Lauren picked it up. 'Granger's Farm, Lauren Foster speaking.'

'Oh hello, Lauren. It's Mrs Cassidy.'

'Hi,' said Lauren, wondering why Mel's

mum was ringing her when Mel was
staying at Jessica's house.

'Is your mum there?'

'Yes, I think she's in her study. I'll just
get her.' Lauren carried the phone
through to her mum's study. 'Mrs
Cassidy's on the phone!'

Her mum took the receiver. 'Hi.'
Lauren was about to leave the room
when she heard her mum's voice change.
'Really?' Mrs Foster sounded alarmed.
'The pony came back on her own?'

Lauren frowned. *Pony? What pony?*

'Of course we'll help,' her mum was
saying. 'I'll get Tim and we'll come right
over.'

'What was that about?' Lauren asked as

her mum put the phone down.

'A friend of the Cassidys went riding
in the woods this afternoon, and her
pony came back without her half an hour
ago. The pony seems fine but the girl
hasn't been seen since. Her mum's
organizing a search party.'

'What is the girl's name?' Lauren said,
her heart beating faster.

'Jo-Ann,' Mrs Foster replied, heading

through to the kitchen.

'Jo-Ann!' Lauren echoed.

'Do you know her?' Mrs Foster asked.

'I've met her in the woods a few times.'
Lauren dug her nails into her palms.
Jo-Ann was in trouble!

'Well, hopefully we'll find her soon,'
said Mrs Foster, peering doubtfully
through the window. It was already
getting dark and it had started to snow
again. 'I'm going to get your dad and
head over to the Cassidys' place. Do you
want to come?'

Lauren hesitated, thinking fast. 'No,' she
said. 'I think I'll stay here.'

'OK. I'll ring you when there's some
news.' Mrs Foster kissed her. 'And try not

to worry, honey. I'm sure we'll find
Jo-Ann.'

Lauren watched her mum getting into
the truck and heading off to the barns.
What should she do?

There was only one answer.

As soon as the truck's headlights
disappeared down the drive, she pulled
on her boots and coat and began to run
down the path to Twilight's field.

'Twilight!' she shouted. 'Twilight!
Quick!'

CHAPTER

Eight

Twilight's whinny reached Lauren long before she could see him. As she raced up to the gate, heart pounding, he trotted over, whickering in delight.

She panted out the words of the Turning Spell. In a flash, Twilight turned into a unicorn.

'Lauren, what's the –'

'Listen,' she interrupted him. 'I've only

turned you into a unicorn because I need your help. Jo-Ann's missing. I think she might have fallen off somewhere in the forest and we need to find her. I want you to use your magic to look into a seeing stone and see where she is.'

Twilight started to speak. 'But –'

'Don't tell me you can't do it!' Lauren burst out, her anger and hurt spilling over. 'I *know* you can. I know you've just been lying to me because you don't want to be my unicorn any more!'

Twilight was astounded. 'What?'

'Just do the magic, Twilight!' Lauren exclaimed furiously. 'Then you can go back to Arcadia! Yes, I know that's what you're planning,' she went on. 'I know you've been visited by a Unicorn Elder to talk about it, but right now I don't care.' Tears burned in her eyes. 'Just help Jo-Ann. Then you can go!'

'But Lauren!' Twilight protested. 'I'm not going anywhere.'

'Don't lie!' Lauren cried. 'I know it's true.'

'It's not!' Twilight insisted. 'It's true a Unicorn Elder did come and ask me to go to Arcadia. She told me I'd been

chosen to be an assistant to the Elders,
but last night, I saw her again and told
her I wouldn't go.' His voice dropped. 'I
told her I couldn't leave you, Lauren.'

Lauren stared at him. 'You're . . . you're
not going back?' she whispered.

Twilight shook his head. 'The Unicorn
Elder told me that if I don't go, I might

lose my unicorn powers for real but I don't care.' He looked at Lauren with his dark eyes. 'You're right. As long as we're together, nothing else matters. I'm your unicorn, Lauren, whether I can do magic or not.'

Lauren swallowed. 'You lied to me,' she said in a shaky voice. 'You told me your

powers were going.'

'I'm sorry,' Twilight mumbled, looking wretched. 'I only did it because I couldn't bear to hurt you. I thought that if I said my magic was fading, you wouldn't mind so much when I went away. But now I'm not going anywhere – I've said no!'

Lauren's mind whirled. *He wasn't going. It had all been a mistake . . .*

Twilight nuzzled her hair. 'Look, we can sort this out later. We should be trying to find Jo-Ann now.'

His words jerked Lauren back to reality. 'You're right!' she exclaimed. Jo-Ann needed their help. 'We need a seeing stone.' Taking hold of his mane, she swung herself on to his back.

'Over by the tree!' Twilight said and he cantered towards the edge of the field. He halted under the large oak tree beside a pinky-grey rock of rose quartz. Twilight bent his head and touched the rock with his horn. 'Help us find Jo-Ann,' he murmured.

There was a burst of purple smoke and the surface of the rock turned into a shimmering mirror. In the mirror, a picture formed of a girl lying in a crumpled heap on a frosty track.

'It's Jo-Ann!' Lauren gasped. 'She's injured! And she must be freezing!' She looked more closely at the picture. 'It's the clearing with the banks!' she said. 'Come on, let's fly there!'

Twilight nodded eagerly. Lauren climbed on to his back and, with a snort, he plunged into the sky.

The wind whipped against Lauren's cheeks as they swooped through the air. She'd been desperate to fly again ever since Twilight told her he was losing his powers, but now she was too worried to enjoy it. Her heart thudded wildly. How badly injured was Jo-Ann? She had been lying so still in the seeing stone. Fear gripped Lauren. 'Faster, Twilight!'

He tossed his head and galloped faster over the trees.

Although the clearing was quite hard to get to along the tracks in the woods,

Twilight got there in no time at all by flying above the treetops. 'There she is!' he cried as they swooped into the clearing.

Jo-Ann was lying at the bottom of the steepest bank, beside a jump made out of branches and logs. Her eyes were closed and her leg was twisted at a strange angle.

'She must have tried that jump!' Lauren gasped.

Twilight landed beside Jo-Ann and Lauren scrambled off his back.

'She's still breathing,' Twilight said in relief.

'Jo-Ann?' Lauren said gently.

The girl didn't move.

Lauren turned to Twilight. 'What do we do?'

'I'll try and help her with my magic.' Twilight bent down until his horn was touching Jo-Ann's leg. Lauren watched as he closed his eyes in concentration. They had used his magic powers before to heal wounds but no one had ever needed it as much as Jo-Ann did now.

Please let this work, Lauren prayed. *Please let Twilight's magic help Jo-Ann.*

Twilight's horn shone even brighter. For a moment nothing happened, but then Lauren saw some of the tension leave Jo-Ann's face, and she shifted so that her leg was lying more naturally. Twilight lightly touched his horn against Jo-Ann's forehead. Again it glowed with magic. A few seconds later, Jo-Ann's eyelids fluttered and she sighed.

'The magic needs some time to work,' Twilight whispered to Lauren. 'Her leg was broken and she's had a bad bang to her head, but I think she'll be OK.'

Lauren's knees felt weak with relief. 'We should get her home. Will it be all right to move her?' She knew it could be dangerous to move someone who was badly injured.

Twilight nodded. 'My magic will protect her.'

'Let's take her to the Cassidys' farm,' Lauren suggested. 'It's closer, and that's where the search party was meeting.'

Twilight nodded and knelt down so that Lauren could lift Jo-Ann on to his back. She was bigger than Lauren and

because she was unconscious it was hard
to get her on to Twilight's back but at last
Lauren managed it. Scrambling up beside
her, she put her arms round her and
Twilight smoothly took off.

As they flew, colour started to return to
Jo-Ann's cheeks. Lauren held on to her
tightly. *Please let Twilight be right*, she
thought, *please let her be OK*.

Suddenly Twilight tensed. 'There are
some people ahead. I can hear their
voices. I'd better fly round another way.
We don't want them to see us.'

Lauren started to nod but then she had
a thought. 'It could be part of the search
party looking for Jo-Ann. I bet they've
come to check the clearing.' She strained

her ears but couldn't hear anything. 'Can you tell who it is, Twilight?'

Hovering in the air, Twilight listened hard. 'I can hear your dad and a few other people. I think one of them's Mrs Cassidy!'

Lauren felt a rush of relief. 'Let's fly down. If I turn you into a pony I can say I rode to the clearing and found Jo-Ann there.'

Twilight nodded and cantered down. As he landed behind some oak trees, Jo-Ann stirred and her eyelids fluttered. Lauren had a feeling that she was turning Twilight back into a pony just in time!

She helped Jo-Ann off Twilight's back

and gently leant her against the trunk of a tree.

'Where am I?' Jo-Ann murmured, still with her eyes closed.

Lauren quickly whispered the words of the Undoing Spell.

There was a purple flash and Jo-Ann's eyes shot open. 'What was that?' she gasped.

'Nothing,' Lauren said as, behind Jo-Ann, Twilight transformed into a pony.

Jo-Ann blinked and stared at her. 'Lauren? Is that you? Where am I?'

'In the woods,' Lauren replied. 'I think you must have fallen off Beauty and been knocked out. Don't worry, there are people coming. They'll be able to help.'

Twilight whinnied loudly and through the trees Lauren heard the sound of voices getting closer. 'We're over here!' she called.

As Twilight whinnied again, Jo-Ann gripped Lauren's arm. 'Where's Beauty? Is she OK?'

'She's at home,' Lauren said. 'She's fine. She went back to the stables without you.'

Jo-Ann rubbed her eyes. 'I can't remember anything. I was riding Beauty

and then . . .' she hesitated. 'I can remember this weird feeling, like I was flying on a horse through the air.'

Lauren hid a smile. 'You must have bumped your head pretty hard!'

Jo-Ann laughed weakly. 'Yeah, flying! As if!'

Just then, the search party arrived. Lauren's dad was with Mrs Cassidy and a few other adults that Lauren didn't know. They looked very relieved indeed to see

Jo-Ann sitting up and talking.

One of them, a woman with short blonde hair, ran forward. 'Jo, honey! Are you OK?'

'I'm fine, Mum,' said Jo-Ann. 'I've just got a terrible headache and my leg hurts a bit. The last thing I remember was being on Beauty. I guess I must have tried to ride too fast down the slope and fallen off. It was a really dumb thing to do. I'm sorry.'

Her mum hugged her hard. 'The most important thing is that you're OK. It's lucky you weren't badly hurt!'

'I'll ring my husband,' said Mrs Cassidy, taking her phone out of her pocket. 'He'll bring the pick-up to take Jo-Ann

home. Then we should let the others
know we've found her.'

Mr Foster hurried over to Lauren.
'What were you doing in the woods?
How did you find Jo-Ann?'

Lauren took a breath. 'Well, after you
and Mum had gone, I realized that Jo-
Ann might be in the clearing we've been
riding in. So I got Twilight and decided
to have a look.' *It's almost the truth*, she
thought. 'I found her lying by the slope,'
she went on. 'I put her on Twilight and
started to bring her home. Then I heard
your voices, so we shouted to you.'

Her dad hugged her. 'Well done.
Though really you shouldn't have gone
out into the woods on your own in the

dark. It would have been best to ring us first.'

'I'm sorry,' Lauren said.

'It's OK.' Her dad smiled. 'It's all worked out fine in the end.'

There was the sound of an engine and headlights appeared through the trees. Jo-Ann's mum and Mrs Cassidy helped Jo-Ann up. 'Time to get you home,' said Mrs Cassidy.

Jo-Ann turned to look at Lauren. 'Thanks for finding me, Lauren.'

Lauren smiled. 'That's OK. See you.'

'Yeah.' Jo-Ann smiled back as her mum helped her towards the truck. She was limping, but her leg wasn't broken like it had been in the clearing. Twilight's magic

had worked!

Mr Foster put an arm round Lauren's shoulders. 'Do you want me to walk back with you?'

'It's OK,' she said. 'You go in the truck. I'll ride Twilight. It's not far and I'll get home faster if I can canter.'

Her dad nodded. 'OK. I know you'll be safe with Twilight.' He patted Twilight's neck. 'Best pony in the world, aren't you, fella?'

Twilight snorted.

'See you at home,' Mr Foster smiled.

He hurried to join the others in the truck. As the sound of the engine faded, Lauren turned to Twilight. Now that all the excitement was over, she realized that they had some talking to do. She said the words of the Turning Spell.

In a second, Twilight was a unicorn again.

For a moment neither of them spoke. When they'd been helping Jo-Ann, everything else had been forgotten – all the unhappiness, all the lies, all the worries about what would happen next. But now they were alone again, everything came flooding back.

Lauren cleared her throat. 'So, you're not going back to Arcadia?'

'No.' Twilight took a breath. 'No, I'm not.'

Their eyes met and they both took a step towards each other, speaking at the same time.

'Oh, Twilight, I felt so . . .'

'I'm sorry, Lauren, I never meant . . .'

They both stopped.

'You go first,' Twilight said.

'No, you,' Lauren told him.

He lifted his muzzle to her face. 'I'm sorry,' he breathed. 'I never meant to hurt you. I only lied about my powers going because I thought it would make things easier for you. I love you, Lauren.'

She swallowed. 'I know. I love you too. But I wish you'd told me the truth all along. When I saw you with that other unicorn in the sky, I thought that you'd been lying because you were planning on going back to Arcadia without telling me. It was awful, the worst feeling ever.' She touched his neck. 'It's kind of my fault though. I should have known better. I should have trusted you.'

'I should have told you the truth.' Twilight sighed. 'I just felt so confused. It's a great honour to be asked to go back to Arcadia. I've never heard of a unicorn saying no.'

Lauren looked at him. 'But you did.'

Twilight nodded. 'For you.'

Lauren rested her forehead against his.
She was remembering what he had told
her before. 'Is it true that if you don't go,
you'll lose your magic powers?'

Twilight nodded. 'That's what the Elder
said. But I don't care. So long as I'm with

you, Lauren, I don't mind giving up my magic.'

Lauren bit her lip. She knew how much his magic meant to him. *I can't make him give it up for me*, she thought. *I can't*. No matter how much it hurt, she had to let him go. 'You . . .' Her voice dropped to a whisper. 'You should go.'

Twilight took a step back. 'What?'

Lauren's heart felt like it was breaking. But she couldn't make him give up his magic. 'Twilight, you have to go back,' she said, tears filling her eyes. 'You're brilliant at using your powers. Look how you helped Jo-Ann tonight. If you were in Arcadia you could help so many people. I can't keep you here.'

'But I don't want to leave you, Lauren,' Twilight said desperately.

'You have to.' A sob burst from her. 'We both know you do.'

'No,' Twilight said, shaking his head in dismay.

Just then, there was the sound of a twig snapping behind them. They swung round in alarm.

A Unicorn Elder was standing in the trees at the side of the clearing. She was much bigger than Twilight, and her silver horn glittered in the moonlight.

Lauren stared at the unicorn in horror, a single thought leaping into her head.

She's come to take Twilight away.

CHAPTER

Ten

The Unicorn Elder stepped forward and bowed her head. 'Hello, Lauren.'

Lauren couldn't speak. She gripped Twilight's mane.

'My name is Sidra,' said the unicorn.

Twilight faced the unicorn bravely. 'I won't go! I won't! I told you –'

'It's all right, Twilight,' Sidra interrupted

him. 'I have not come to take you away.'
Her beautiful eyes shone. 'Quite the
opposite, in fact.'

Twilight stared at her, puzzled.

'What do you mean?' Lauren asked.

Sidra looked from Lauren to Twilight.
'I, and some of the other Elders, have
been watching tonight as you helped the
injured girl. It made us realize that
although the mirror has chosen Twilight
to come back to Arcadia and train as an
Elder's assistant, now is not the time. So,
Twilight, we have decided that you can
stay. It is clear you can do a lot of good
with Lauren. As much, maybe even more,
than you could do with us in Arcadia.'

'I can stay!' Twilight breathed.

'Will he still have his magic powers?'
Lauren wondered.

Sidra nodded.

'Oh, Twilight!' Lauren gasped, throwing
her arms round his neck.

Sidra smiled. 'You love each other and
deserve to be together. The Unicorn
Elders are sure you will do many good
things.'

'Oh, we will!' Lauren promised. 'At
least we'll try to, won't we, Twilight?'

'Definitely!' he said. 'Thank you! Thank
you so much!'

The unicorn bowed her head again.
'We thank you for all the good deeds you
have already done, and wish you good
luck for the future.' She touched her
magnificent silver horn to Twilight's

forehead and then to Lauren's. Lauren felt
a tingly warm feeling spread through her.

Magic! she thought.

The unicorn blinked warmly at her.
'You are a very special unicorn friend,
Lauren. Very special indeed.'

Lauren felt overwhelmed with pride
and happiness.

'And now I must go,' Sidra said, tossing
back her mane. 'Come, you may fly
beside me some of the way if you wish.'

'Yes, please!' Lauren said and Twilight
nodded eagerly.

Lauren climbed on to his back and
twisted her fingers in his silky mane as he
and the Elder plunged into the sky. The
stars whizzed past in a glittering stream

and the wind whipped Lauren's hair back from her face. She didn't think she had ever flown so fast or so high! She laughed out loud as Twilight tossed his head in delight and galloped even faster beside the snow-white Unicorn Elder with the glittering silver horn.

'I must leave you here!' Sidra said, halting and rearing up against the dark sky. 'Goodbye, Lauren! Goodbye, Twilight! Good luck!'

'Goodbye!' they called.

And with a flash of purple light, Sidra disappeared.

'Oh, wow!' Lauren gasped. 'Wasn't that fun!'

'The best!' Twilight agreed.

'I guess we should go home now,' Lauren sighed. 'Dad will be wondering where I am.'

Circling in the sky, they flew back towards Granger's Farm. They landed at the edge of the woods so Lauren could turn Twilight back to a pony in case her

mum and dad were looking out for
them.

Just before saying the words of the
spell, she pressed her cheek against his
neck. There was one more thing she
wanted to clear up. 'You know that time I
overheard you saying, "I have to tell her"?
You really didn't mean me, did you?'

'No,' Twilight said. 'I was thinking
about Sidra. I knew I had to tell her that
I couldn't leave you.' He turned and blew
gently in her hair. 'I'm sorry you ever
thought I would.'

'I'm sorry too,' Lauren said. 'I should
have trusted you more.'

'And I should have trusted you,'
Twilight replied. 'If I'd told you the truth

from the start, you wouldn't have been so upset.'

'I probably would have,' Lauren admitted, thinking honestly about how she would have reacted if he'd told her he'd been asked to go back to Arcadia. 'But at least we could have talked it through together. Like best friends.' She stroked his nose. 'So from now on, no more secrets. Promise?'

'No more secrets,' Twilight agreed.

Lauren smiled and said the words of the Undoing Spell.

In a flash, Twilight was a pony again. Looking at him standing there, with his fluffy grey coat and pricked-up ears, Lauren felt a rush of love. He was her

pony, her unicorn, but most of all he was
her best friend.

Putting an arm round his neck, she
kissed him. 'Come on,' she said happily.
'Let's go home.'

Do you love magic, unicorns and fairies?

Join the sparkling

My Secret Unicorn

fan club today!

It's FREE!

You will receive a sparkle pack, including:

Stickers   **Badge**

Membership card   **Glittery pencil**

Plus four Linda Chapman newsletters every year,
packed full of fun, games, news and competitions.
And look out for a special card on your birthday!

How to join:

Visit mysecretunicorn.co.uk and enter your details

Send your name, address, date of birth* and email address (if you have one) to:

**Linda Chapman Fan Club, Puffin Marketing,
80 Strand, London, WC2R 0RL**

Your details will be kept by Puffin only for the purpose of sending information regarding Linda Chapman
and other relevant Puffin books. It will not be passed on to any third parties.
You will receive your free introductory pack within 28 days

*If you are under 13, you must get permission from a parent or guardian

Notice to parent/guardian of children under 13 years old: Please add the following to their email/letter including
your name and signature: I consent to my child/ward submitting his/her personal details as above.

My Secret Unicorn

When Lauren recites a secret spell, Twilight turns into a beautiful unicorn with magical powers! Together Lauren and Twilight learn how to use their magic to help their friends.

Look out for more *My Secret Unicorn* adventures:

Stronger Than Magic
A Special Friend
A Winter Wish
A Touch of Magic

Have you read them all?